For Victoria and Alastair

Published by Bloomsbury, New York and London
Distributed to the trade by Holtzbrinck Publishers
Library of Congress Cataloging-in-Publication Data
available upon request

ISBN 1-58234-935-5

First U.S. Edition 2004

1 3 5 7 9 10 8 6 4 2

Bloomsbury USA Children's Books
175 Fifth Avenue
New York, NY 10010

Grandma's Beach

Rosalind Beardshaw

BLOOMSBURY
CHILDREN'S
BOOKS

Emily and her mom are going to the beach.
"Hooray!" shouted Emily.
"Don't forget your sunhat," Mom said, smiling.

As they packed the car,
Mom's phone rang.

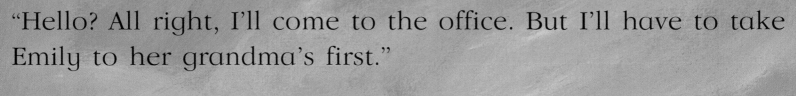

"Hello? All right, I'll come to the office. But I'll have to take Emily to her grandma's first."

But Grandma doesn't live at the seaside, Emily thought sadly.

Emily's mom drove quickly to Grandma's house.
"Hello Emily, what a lovely surprise,"
said Grandma.

"Hello Grandma ... I really wanted to go to the beach," said Emily quietly.

"Well, go and put your beach things on and we'll see what we can do."

"Bye Emily. I'll pick you up later," said Mom.

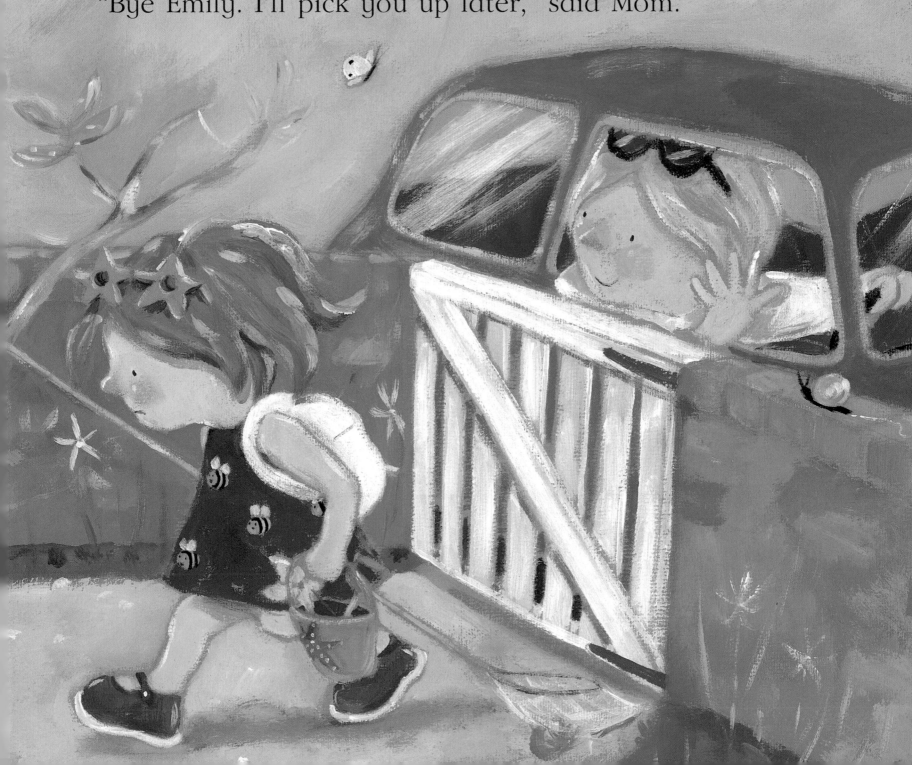

While Emily was changing ...
Grandma got busy!

"Come on, Emily, everything's ready ..."

And when Emily came outside ...

"Quick—bring your fishing net to the rock pool, Emily. I think I saw something."

"It's a fish!"

Then Grandma had another idea.
"Come on, Emily, let's build a sandcastle."

"We'll see about that!" said Grandma.

"Watch out Emily, the tide's coming in!"
"But Grandma, there's no water!"
"That's what you think!"

"Let's sunbathe and dry off," laughed Grandma.

Soon it was time for lunch.
"Fish and chips," said Grandma.

"Mmmmm ... delicious!" said
Emily, all covered in ketchup.

"Now close your eyes, Emily, I've got a surprise for you," said Grandma.

"Look at you two!" said Mom as she came into the garden.
"I'm sorry we couldn't go to the beach today, Emily.
Shall we go tomorrow?"

"That's ok, Mom, I like Grandma's beach best!" said Emily.